Leona
the Unicorn Fairy

by Daisy Meadows

ORCHARD BOOKS

www.rainbowmagic.co.uk

Jack Frost's
Ice Castle

Meadows

Amphitheatre

The Labyrinth

Cabins

Maze of tunnels

Waterfall

Hills

There are seven special animals,
Who live in Fairyland.
They use their magic powers
To help others where they can.

A dragon, black cat, firebird,
A seahorse and snow swan too,
A unicorn and ice bear -
I know just what to do.

I'll lock them in my castle
And never let them out.
The world will turn more miserable,
Of that, I have no doubt...

Contents

spooked!

"Isn't this great, Kirsty?" Rachel Walker twisted round in her saddle to smile at her best friend, Kirsty Tate. "I'd only ever been horseriding once or twice before, but now I just love it!" And Rachel patted her chestnut pony, Sparkle.

"Me too," agreed Kirsty, who was on a beautiful black pony behind Rachel.

The girls had been having riding
lessons ever since they arrived at camp,
but this was the first time they'd been on
a trail ride through the forest. "I think it's
because Sparkle and Tansy are so sweet.
They don't mind if we do something
wrong!"

"Keep following the trail, everyone,"
called Susan, their riding instructor, from
the back of the line. There were several
other campers on
ponies in front of
and behind
Kirsty and
Rachel. "It
will lead us
back to
the camp
eventually."

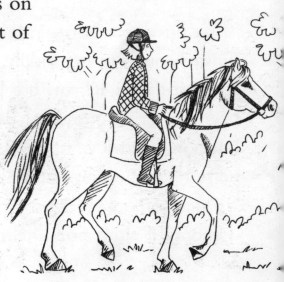

"I can't believe we've only got a day and a half left at camp," Rachel sighed as the ponies ambled on through the forest. It was cool and shady under the trees, but beams of sunlight dappled the grass here and there. "We've had *such* a good time, haven't we, Kirsty? We've tried hiking, orienteering, bird-watching and caving, and we've made some great friends."

But Kirsty wasn't really listening. She was staring around, peering through the trees on either side of the trail.

"Sorry, Rachel," she said quickly. "I was just seeing if I could spot anything unusual…"

Rachel smiled. She knew exactly what Kirsty was looking for! On the day the girls arrived at camp, the King and Queen of Fairyland had asked for their help.

Kirsty and Rachel
had discovered that
Jack Frost and his
goblin servants
had kidnapped
seven magical
young animals from the

Magical Animal Fairies. These animals
had the power to spread the kind of
magical qualities that every human and
fairy could possess – the magic of
imagination, luck, humour, friendship,
compassion, healing and courage. It was
the fairies' job to train the Magical
Animals for a whole year to make sure
they knew how to use their magic
properly. Then the animals would use
their incredible powers to bring happiness
to both the human and the fairy worlds.

But Jack Frost was determined to disrupt the Magical Animals' training because he didn't want *anyone*, humans or fairies, to be happy. So, with the help of his goblins, Jack Frost had stolen the animals from Fairyland and imprisoned them in his Ice Castle. But the young animals had managed to escape and had hidden themselves away in the human world. Jack Frost had sent his goblins to find them, but the Magical Animal Fairies had asked Rachel and Kirsty to help them track down the animals and return them safely to Fairyland.

"Remember what Queen Titania says, Kirsty," Rachel whispered. "It doesn't always help to look for magic. You must let the magic find *you!*"

"I know," Kirsty replied, "But it's *so* difficult! I just want to find Leona's unicorn and Caitlin's ice bear. I'm worried about them because they haven't learned how to use their magical powers properly yet."

"We're doing OK, though," Rachel pointed out. "We've already found Ashley's dragon, Lara's little black cat, Erin's firebird, Rihanna's seahorse and Sophia's snow swan."

"That's true," Kirsty said with a smile. "Let's just enjoy the trail ride and wait for the magic to come to us!"

Rachel nodded. "Look, Kirsty, there's another fox," she said, catching a glimpse of russet brown between the trees. "That makes two we've seen now."

"Yes, as well as three rabbits and six squirrels!" Kirsty replied. "There's lots of wildlife around here, isn't there?"

Suddenly, without any warning at all, the pony in front of Rachel and Kirsty gave a frightened little neigh and reared upwards. Lauren, the camper riding the pony, gasped with fright.

"Quick, Rachel!" Kirsty cried urgently, spotting a side path to her left. "Down here!"

Swiftly Kirsty and Rachel pulled Tansy and Sparkle off the trail and down the side path to avoid a collision.

Meanwhile Lauren got her pony, Sky, under control again.

"Are you all right, girls?" called Susan, trotting towards them. "Looks like Sky got spooked by something."

"I'm fine," said Lauren, patting Sky's neck. Rachel and Kirsty nodded in agreement.

"Good thinking, you two," Susan went on, smiling at them. "You got your ponies out of the way just in time."

As the riders moved on again, Kirsty and Rachel turned their ponies around to rejoin the main path. But then, Kirsty saw a sudden flash of bright green in the undergrowth around her. Immediately she turned to her friend.

"Rachel!" Kirsty gasped. "I just saw something green – and it definitely wasn't anything leafy!"

"Do you think it was a goblin?" Rachel whispered, alarmed. "Maybe there's more wildlife in this forest than we thought!"

"It *could* have been a goblin that scared Lauren's pony," Kirsty suggested.

"We'll check it out," Rachel said. "Let's hang back and join the end of the line."

The girls waited until the other campers had ridden past, and then they trotted back onto the trail some distance behind them. They kept a sharp look-out for goblins, but didn't see anything.

Then Rachel heard a rustling in the bushes. Before she could say anything to Kirsty, two goblins jumped out onto the path, right in front of them!

The Unicorn Appears

"Oh!" Kirsty gasped, quickly bringing Tansy to a halt. Rachel did the same with Sparkle.

The biggest goblin nudged the smaller one and pointed at the two ponies.

"Is one of those a unicorn?" he whispered in a loud voice.

Rachel glanced at Kirsty. These goblins must be looking for Leona's unicorn, one of the missing Magical Animals!

The smallest goblin looked disgusted. "Are you stupid?" he demanded. "These are ponies, not unicorns! Unicorns have a horn on top of their heads—"

"Don't call me stupid!" the other goblin screeched furiously.

"Well, you *are* stupid!" the smallest goblin yelled. "Whoever heard of a unicorn without a horn?"

Arguing loudly, the two goblins began shoving each other.

Kirsty was alarmed. The path was too narrow for them to get past the fighting goblins, and they were coming closer to the girls' ponies.

"Look out!" Kirsty called.

The biggest goblin pushed the smaller one in front of Rachel's pony. Sparkle gave a loud, startled neigh and reared up. The goblins yelped in alarm and shot off through the undergrowth.

"It's OK, Sparkle!" Rachel gasped, trying to get the frightened pony under control. But Sparkle bolted off at top speed through the trees, with Rachel clinging desperately to the reins.

"Oh no!" Kirsty cried, horrified. "Hold on, Rachel!" And she urged Tansy after them.

Rachel's heart was pounding anxiously as Sparkle galloped through the forest. She had to keep ducking to avoid low branches, and she was very worried that either she'd fall off the pony or that a branch would hit her.

"Whoa, Sparkle!" she called.
Remembering what they'd been taught
in their riding lessons, Rachel squeezed
Sparkle's flanks with her legs and pulled
back on the reins. But unfortunately
Sparkle slowed down and stopped too
quickly. Rachel wasn't expecting this,
and she flew right over the pony's head.

"Rachel!" Kirsty shouted,
cantering up behind
Sparkle just in time
to see her
friend go
sailing
through
the air.

To Kirsty's relief, she saw that Rachel had landed on a soft, springy patch of moss on the forest floor. Jumping quickly down from Tansy, Kirsty rushed over to her friend.

"Are you OK, Rachel?" Kirsty asked, kneeling down beside her. She could see that Rachel was holding her arm, looking rather shaken.

"I'm fine, except I think I've sprained my wrist," Rachel replied, wincing. "It hurts a lot."

"I'll run after Susan and get help," Kirsty said, glancing round. "They can't have got much further up the trail."

But at that moment, a gleam of pure, dazzling white among the trees caught Kirsty's eye. It appeared to be coming straight towards them.

"Rachel, look!" Kirsty gasped in wonder as the white shape came closer. "It's a *unicorn*."

"It's Leona's missing Magical Animal!" Rachel whispered, her eyes wide.

The beautiful young unicorn came trotting through the trees towards them. He was about the size of a Shetland pony, and his coat was gleaming white. He had shining golden hooves and a twisted golden horn on his head.

The unicorn stopped a few metres from Rachel and Kirsty. He lowered his snow-white head, shaking his long mane, and suddenly a shower of golden glitter burst from his horn. It flew through the air and encircled Rachel's injured wrist like a dazzling bracelet.

The girls could hardly believe their eyes. A few seconds later, the glitter began to dissolve in a sparkling mist.

"Rachel! Kirsty! Where are you?"

"That's Susan," Kirsty said as they heard the sound of a horse's hooves. "She's looking for us."

The unicorn's ears pricked up. Quickly he turned and galloped off through the trees.

"Oh, please come back!" Rachel called after him. She turned to Kirsty, looking worried. "However will we find him again, Kirsty?

"I don't know." Kirsty frowned. "Let's just hope the goblins don't find him first!"

Leona's Lollipop

Kirsty put out her hand to help Rachel to her feet. As she stood up, Rachel suddenly gave a gasp.

"Is your wrist hurting?" Kirsty asked sympathetically.

Rachel shook her head. "No, that's just it," she replied, bending her wrist this way and that. "It's all better!"

"I've just remembered," Kirsty said excitedly. "The unicorn's magical power is healing. He must have healed your wrist with the glitter from his horn!"

At that moment Susan rode through the trees towards them.

"Are you OK, girls?" she asked, dismounting quickly and coming over to them. "We suddenly realised that you weren't with us on the trail."

"Sparkle got spooked and bolted," Rachel explained. She hoped the goblins weren't anywhere around. It would be a disaster if Susan spotted them because no one was meant to know that Fairyland existed. "But I'm fine."

"Lucky you were wearing your riding-hat, or your injuries could have been a lot worse," Susan said, as she checked Rachel over.

Rachel winked at Kirsty. "Luck and the healing touch of a unicorn!" she whispered, as Susan went to check Sparkle for injuries, too.

"Right, time to get back to camp,"
Susan said briskly. "I think you've had
enough excitement for one day, and
your free-time session is coming up,
so you won't want to miss that."

Reluctantly, Rachel and Kirsty climbed
back onto their ponies.

"I don't want
to leave the
unicorn in
the forest
all alone,"
Kirsty said
anxiously
to Rachel
as they
followed Susan
back to the trail. "Not
with the goblins around!"

"Let's come back and search for the
unicorn when we've put Sparkle and
Tansy in the stables," Rachel suggested.

Back at the camp Rachel and Kirsty
led their ponies into their shared stall and
carefully began to brush them down. The
stable door was open and, as Rachel and
Kirsty brushed their ponies' manes, they
heard voices outside.

"Do you know if any ponies have escaped from the stables, Katie?" someone asked. Kirsty and Rachel recognised the voice. It was Emma, one of their dorm-mates. "I think I saw a small white pony heading towards the amphitheatre just now."

"Really? You must be seeing things!" Katie said teasingly. "There aren't any white ponies here."

Kirsty and Rachel glanced at each other in alarm. The amphitheatre was a round, open-air theatre where the campers could put on shows and perform plays.

So the unicorn had come to the camp!

"That's what I thought." Emma sounded very puzzled. "What's *really* weird though is that it looked like the pony had a twisted horn on its head!"

"Maybe it's a unicorn?" Katie suggested, laughing.

Emma laughed too. "It's probably just a practical joke," she said. "The campers and counsellors have been playing funny tricks on each other all week, haven't they? I found a plastic frog inside one of my wellies this morning!"

Rachel turned to Kirsty as the other two girls walked away, still laughing.

"I think the unicorn must have followed us back to camp!" Rachel exclaimed. "We *have* to find him before someone realises he's a *real* unicorn."

"Or he's captured by the goblins," Kirsty added.

Quickly, Rachel and Kirsty gave Tansy and Sparkle their buckets of oats, as well as a few carrots for a treat. Then they rushed out of the stall.

"Rachel?" Susan popped out of one of the other stalls as they went by. "I want you to stop by the first-aid cabin and see Elizabeth, the camp nurse."

"But I'm fine," Rachel insisted.

"It can't do any harm to be sure, can it?" Susan said kindly. "Off you go."

Rachel's face fell as Susan went back into the stall.

"I hope this doesn't take too long," she said anxiously as she and Kirsty hurried off to the first-aid cabin.

"Ah, there you are, Rachel." Elizabeth was at her desk rolling up bandages when the girls knocked and went in. She was young and friendly with a snow-white uniform and long red hair pinned neatly back. "Let's take a look at you. Any bumps or bruises?"

Rachel shook her head.

"Well, you seem fine," Elizabeth remarked a few minutes later with a smile. "I think you can safely go off and enjoy the rest of the afternoon."

"Thanks, Elizabeth," Rachel said, jumping eagerly to her feet. "Sorry to have wasted your time."

"Oh, it was nice to have something to do," Elizabeth replied. "I usually see a dozen or more campers every day with various scrapes and bruises, but you're the only ones I've seen so far today." She picked up another roll of bandages. "So I decided to tidy my medicine cupboard instead."

"That's because of Leona's unicorn," Kirsty whispered to Rachel as they went to the door of the cabin. "His healing powers mean the campers don't need the nurse!"

"Help yourself to a lollipop from my jar on your way out, girls," Elizabeth called.

There was a big glass jar of brightly coloured lollipops on a shelf near the door. As Rachel lifted it down, she noticed that the jar was glowing strangely.

"What's going on?" Rachel whispered to Kirsty, her eyes wide with amazement as she unscrewed the lid.

Kirsty looked excited. She put her hand into the jar and pulled out a red strawberry-flavoured lollipop. Clinging to the top of it was a tiny fairy!

Twisty on the Loose

Kirsty just about
managed not to
cry out in surprise. She
and Rachel smiled down at
the fairy, who wore wide-
legged blue trousers, a matching
shrug and a starry gold belt. Her
long blonde hair was tied up in a
ponytail.

"Hello, girls!" the fairy called in a low
voice, her eyes twinkling. "I'm so glad
I've found you! Remember me? I'm
Leona the Unicorn Fairy."

"Hello, Leona," Rachel and Kirsty whispered back.

Quickly the girls went out of the first-aid cabin, Kirsty carrying the lollipop.

"As you know, I'm looking for my unicorn, Twisty," Leona explained. "I thought he might be attracted to the first-aid cabin because he has special healing powers." She looked anxiously at Rachel and Kirsty. "Have you seen him?"

"Yes, but not here," Rachel told Leona.

And quickly she explained how Twisty
had appeared in the forest and healed
her injured wrist.

"But now we think Twisty is right here
in the camp!" Kirsty added. "Emma,
our dorm-mate, saw him near the
amphitheatre. But don't worry, Leona,
she thought it was some sort of joke."

Leona looked relieved.
"We'd better get
to the
amphitheatre
right away!"
she said. She
dived into
Kirsty's
pocket out of
sight, and the
girls hurried off.

The amphitheatre was at the edge of
the camp. As they approached it, Rachel
blinked several times in surprise. She
could see human-sized fairies dancing
around the stage wearing floaty white
dresses and with gauzy wings on their
shoulders.

"They're not *real* fairies, Rachel,"
Kirsty said with a grin. "They're just
campers in costume! Look, one of them
is Catherine from our dorm."

"You're right," Rachel agreed. "For a minute there I thought we had some visitors from Fairyland!"

A Fairy King and Queen, wearing golden crowns, were also dancing amongst the fairies. As the girls got closer to the stage, Kirsty did a double take. Was that a *goblin* skipping along next to the Fairy Queen? But when Kirsty looked again, there was no one there.

"I've got goblins on the brain!" Kirsty thought, shaking her head.

"Katrina," Rachel called to a camper who was watching the dancers. "What's going on?"

"Oh, this is a rehearsal for Shakespeare's play, *A Midsummer Night's Dream*," Katrina explained.

At that moment another camper called Tom wandered past. He heard what Katrina was saying and looked confused.

"Hey, Katrina, there isn't a *unicorn* in the play, is there?" he asked.

Rachel and Kirsty exchanged glances as Katrina shook her head.

"No, why?"

Tom laughed. "Someone must have attached a horn to a Shetland pony's head for a joke then!" he replied. "I just saw it leave the amphitheatre and trot towards the clubhouse."

"Well, there aren't supposed to be any goblins in this play either." Katrina shrugged. "But I've seen two campers dressed up as goblins this afternoon!"

Rachel and Kirsty both gasped with horror. So the goblins were at the camp too!

"I even overheard one of the actors refuse to take off his goblin costume," Katrina said with a laugh. "Some people really get into their parts!"

"We'd better go straight
to the clubhouse," Leona
whispered, popping her
head out of Kirsty's pocket
as the girls hurried off. "The
goblins are on Twisty's trail too. We *must*
find him before they do!"

Rachel and Kirsty ran to the
clubhouse. They had a quick look around
outside, but couldn't see Twisty.

"What are we going to do, Rachel?"
Kirsty asked desperately. "We can't run
around the camp all day!"

"Let's ask inside if anyone's seen
anything," Rachel suggested.

The girls rushed into the clubhouse.
Some of the campers were playing
ping pong and pool while others
watched a movie on TV.

Rachel went over to the boys playing pool. "Sorry to bother you," she said, "but have you seen a pony dressed up to look like a unicorn today?"

"I did," said one of the boys. "When I was playing football."

"What happened?" Rachel asked eagerly.

"Well, I fell over and skinned my knees," the boy explained. "I had to come off the pitch and that pony was standing there watching me. Then it shook its mane and showered glitter over me!" The boy laughed. "I guess someone was trying to trick me into thinking it was a magic unicorn!"

Kirsty and Rachel glanced down at the boy's knees. They didn't look badly grazed at all.

"Maybe the unicorn helped heal the boy, just like he did for you, Rachel," Kirsty whispered.

"I saw the pretend unicorn down by the dock at the lake," another boy at the pool table added. "It looks really realistic! I tried to get a closer look, but he trotted off."

Rachel and Kirsty hurried out of the clubhouse.

"So Twisty could be in *two* places," Rachel said as Leona popped out of Kirsty's pocket. "The sports pitch or the lake."

"If we choose the wrong one, we might miss him," Leona pointed out anxiously.

"Maybe we should split up," suggested Kirsty. "Leona could go to the lake because it's further away and flying will be quicker. Rachel and I can search the sports pitch."

Leona nodded. "Good thinking, Kirsty," she said. "I'll meet you back at the stables in fifteen minutes."

And Leona rose up into the air and zoomed away, her blonde hair flying.

"I don't like being away from Leona, but we *have* to find Twisty before someone realises he's a real unicorn," Rachel sighed, as she and Kirsty dashed off.

"Or before the goblins find him!" Kirsty added.

The girls raced to the sports pitch and began to search around. But to their disappointment, Twisty wasn't there.

"What now?" Rachel asked.

"I suppose we'd better head back to the stables to meet Leona," Kirsty began. But then she broke off as a flash of white in the forest that bordered the sports pitch caught her eye.

"Rachel!" Kirsty cried. "It's Twisty!"

A Ransom Note

"Careful!" Rachel whispered. She gazed at the unicorn who was grazing on the grass between the trees. "We mustn't frighten him."

The girls sneaked across the pitch and up to the unicorn. As they tiptoed towards him, Rachel wondered how they could catch him and take him back to Leona. Then suddenly she realised she still had a carrot in her pocket from feeding

their ponies earlier. She took it out and
showed it silently to Kirsty, who nodded.

"Here, Twisty," Rachel called, holding
the carrot a little way from the
unicorn's nose.

Twisty raised
his head and
sniffed the
carrot.
Rachel
moved
away a
little and
the unicorn
walked after her,
his beautiful dark
eyes fixed on the carrot just in front of
him.

Rachel led Twisty through the forest,

then took a back route towards the stables so that they would be less likely to bump into other campers. Kirsty went in front, keeping a sharp look-out to make sure no one else was about.

When they reached the stables, both girls sighed with relief. They patted Twisty, who shook his mane and gave a little neigh.

"Thank you for healing my wrist today, Twisty," Rachel said, feeding the carrot to the unicorn.

"I wonder where Leona is?" Kirsty said with a frown, glancing around as Twisty crunched up his carrot. Suddenly she spotted a piece of paper stuck to the door of the stables. "What's that, Rachel?"

"It looks like a note," Rachel replied. "What does it say?"

The note was in shaky handwriting
in green ink. It read:

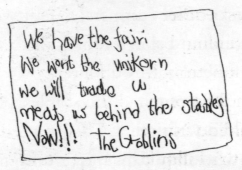

We have the fairi
We wont the unikorn
we will trade u
meat us behind the stables
Now!!! The Goblins

"I don't believe it!" Rachel cried. "The
goblins aren't smart enough to catch
Leona."

"Or *any* fairy!" Kirsty agreed. "It
might be a trap. But we'd better go and
meet them, just in case."

Quickly the girls led Twisty around
the back of the stables. They held on
tightly to the unicorn, afraid that the
goblins might pounce and try to
steal him.

The two goblins who'd
spooked Sparkle in
the forest earlier
were standing by
the ponies' trough.
The smallest one
was holding Nurse
Elizabeth's lollipop
jar. As Rachel, Kirsty
and Twisty came closer,
the goblin shook the jar. It
sparkled in the sun like magic fairy dust.

"Oh no!" Rachel whispered to Kirsty.
"Maybe the goblins *have* captured Leona
in that big jar!"

But Kirsty shook her head. "No, Leona
would use her magic to escape, wouldn't
she?" she replied. "It could just be
something else sparkling inside the jar."

The goblin holding the lollipop jar
turned his back towards Rachel and
Kirsty.

"I'm trapped, girls!" he
called in a high-pitched,
squeaky voice. "Help
me! I mean,
please in a
sparkly, fairy
way!"

Rachel and
Kirsty tried not
to laugh. It was
really obvious that
the goblin was only
pretending to have Leona!

"Hand over that unicorn!" the other
goblin demanded, stepping forward, "and
we'll let your fairy friend go."

At that moment Rachel and Kirsty noticed a twinkling light whizzing through the air towards the goblins. It was Leona! Now the girls *knew* the goblins were bluffing.

"We know you don't have Leona," Rachel said firmly.

"We *do* have her!" The goblin stamped his foot in a rage. "We captured her when she was flying towards the lake."

"And we know she's not with you," the goblin with the jar said triumphantly, "Or the unicorn wouldn't still be here!"

"But *we* know where Leona is," Kirsty said, and she and Rachel both pointed above the goblins' heads.

"Don't try to trick us!" the goblin with the jar jeered. "We've been fooled by you before. Now, give us the unicorn!"

Ponies to the Rescue

Suddenly Leona swooped down, waving cheekily at the goblins. They shrieked with surprise.

"Get her!" the biggest goblin roared.

Quickly, the other goblin unscrewed the jar. He pulled out a handful of glitter and tossed it at Leona. The fairy was forced to dart and dodge around to avoid the sparkles.

"We have to help Leona!" Kirsty
gasped. "Keep hold of Twisty, Rachel!"

Rachel nodded. Immediately Kirsty
dashed forward. She had to
distract the goblins
somehow. As the
goblin threw
another shower
of sparkles at
Leona, Kirsty
rushed over to
Tansy's and
Sparkle's stall.

"Tansy, Sparkle!" she called.

When the ponies saw Kirsty, they
immediately stuck their heads out of the
open top of the door to be stroked. They
neighed happily and the goblins almost
jumped out of their skins.

"Help!" shouted the biggest goblin in terror. "It's those scary ponies again!"

The smallest goblin also gave a yell of surprise. He dropped the lollipop jar, spilling glitter on the ground. Kirsty snatched the jar up.

But as Leona headed towards Twisty, the biggest goblin made one last attempt to catch her. He gave a giant leap, but Leona slipped neatly through his fingers. The goblin sailed through the air and landed with a thud in a pile of horse manure.

"Yuk, gross!" sniggered the smallest goblin.

"Here, Twisty!" Leona called, holding out her arms as she flew towards the unicorn.

Smiling, Rachel released Twisty. He cantered upwards and bounded through the air to Leona. As he did so, he shrank down to his tiny, fairy-size again.

"It's so good to see you again, Twisty!" Leona declared, giving him a hug. Then she jumped onto his back. They zoomed upwards out of the reach of the smallest goblin, who stood staring sulkily up at them.

"Oh, my ankle hurts!" the goblin on
the ground moaned.

Twisty immediately
circled in the air
and hovered
over the goblin.
Then a shower
of glitter burst from
the unicorn's golden horn
and encircled the goblin's injured ankle.

"It's all better!" the goblin said in
amazement, jumping to his feet. Looking
sheepish, he glanced up at Leona and
Twisty. "Thanks," he mumbled.

"Come on, let's go," the smallest goblin
snapped. "I'm fed up with pesky fairies
and silly girls who spoil all our plans!"

"Me too," the other one agreed as they
stomped off.

"Girls, you've done it again!" Leona said happily. "Because of you, almost all our Magical Animals are safely back in Fairyland, and can start their training again. We can never thank you enough – but thank you, anyway!"

"Goodbye," the girls called as Leona and Twisty disappeared in a flourish of fairy sparkles.

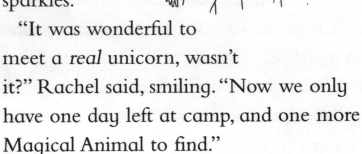

"It was wonderful to meet a *real* unicorn, wasn't it?" Rachel said, smiling. "Now we only have one day left at camp, and one more Magical Animal to find."

"Yes, Caitlin's ice bear," Kirsty replied. "But that's the problem. The ice bear's special power is courage." She looked solemnly at Rachel. "So, while he's missing, will we be able to find the courage to take on the goblins?"

The Magical Animal Fairies

Leona the Unicorn Fairy has got her
Magical Animal back! Now Rachel
and Kirsty must help...

Caitlin the Ice Bear Fairy

Frosty Sparkles!

"I can't believe it's the last day of our holiday already," Kirsty Tate said sadly as she finished packing her bag and zipped it shut. She gazed around the cosy wooden cabin where she and her best friend, Rachel Walker, had spent the week with four other girls. They'd been staying at an Adventure Camp and had taken part in all sorts of activities – exploring caves, canoeing, horseriding… as well as making some very special fairy friends too!

The holiday was almost at an end now,

and their room-mates had packed their things ready to go home. Only Kirsty and Rachel were left in the cabin.

"We've had such brilliant adventures this week," Rachel said, smiling as she thought about them.

Kirsty put on her coat. "Well, the holiday isn't over just yet," she reminded Rachel. "We've got High Hill to climb in a few minutes…and we've got to find the last Magical Animal, too."

Rachel nodded, an anxious expression appearing on her face. "Oh, I hope we do spot the little ice bear," she said. "I hate thinking of her being lost and alone."

"Or caught by Jack Frost's goblins," Kirsty added. "We can't let that happen."

It was rather cold outdoors, so Rachel grabbed their hats and scarves. "Come on," she said. "The sooner we get out there and start looking, the better!"

Unknown to everyone else at the holiday camp, Kirsty and Rachel had been having some extra-special adventures… helping the Magical Animal Fairies find their missing animals! Nasty Jack Frost had stolen them, but the clever animals had found a way to escape from his Ice Castle into the human world, where they'd been lost ever since. So far, the two girls had helped the fairies track down a baby dragon, a magic black cat, a young firebird, a seahorse, snow swan and unicorn. But there was still the ice-bear cub left to find…

Calling all Rainbow Magic fans

– the fairies need YOUR help!

Wicked Jack Frost has stolen

7 precious, glittering Jewel Fairy wands

and hidden them in 7 secret locations all over the countryside.

For your chance to WIN one of the 7 magical wands
AND to feature in a Rainbow Magic book
you must solve the clues in our Rainbow Magic Treasure Hunt!

To take part, all you have to do is:

1) Buy a copy of the special £1 Treasure Hunt edition of
Hannah the Happy Ever After Fairy (in shops from July 2009),
which contains a secret code.

2) Log on to **www.rainbowmagic.co.uk**, enter the special code
and select the region nearest to where you live.

3) Download your own special Rainbow Magic Treasure Map
and get your first Treasure Hunt clue telling you how to begin!

The first clue will be on the website on **Friday 3 July 2009**
and the Fun Day Fairies will be revealing a clue
every Friday for 7 weeks until **Friday 14 August 2009**,
when the last clue will be revealed.

Good Luck!

The Magical Animal Fairies

Win Rainbow Magic goodies!

In every book in the Magical Animal Fairies series
(books 71-77) there is a hidden picture of a pawprint with a secret
letter in it. Find all seven letters and re-arrange them to make
a special Magical Animal Fairies word, then send it to us. Each
month we will put the entries into a draw and select one winner
to receive a Rainbow Magic sparkly T-shirt and goody bag!

Send your entry on a postcard to Rainbow Magic Magical Animal
Fairies Competition, Orchard Books, 338 Euston Road, London
NW1 3BH. Australian readers should write to Hachette Children's
Books, Level 17/207 Kent Street, Sydney, NSW 2000.
New Zealand readers should write to Rainbow Magic Competition,
4 Whetu Place, Mairangi Bay, Auckland, NZ. Don't forget to
include your name and address. Only one entry per child.
Final draw: 30th April 2010.

Have you checked out the

website at:
www.rainbowmagic.co.uk

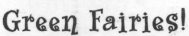

Look out for the

Green Fairies!

NICOLE
THE BEACH FAIRY
978-1-40830-474-7

ISABELLA
THE AIR FAIRY
978-1-40830-475-4

EDIE
THE GARDEN FAIRY
978-1-40830-476-1

CORAL
THE REEF FAIRY
978-1-40830-477-8

LILY
THE RAINFOREST FAIRY
978-1-40830-478-5

MILLY
THE RIVER FAIRY
978-1-40830-480-8

CARRIE
THE SNOW CAP FAIRY
978-1-40830-479-2

Available
September 2009